FISKE PUBLIC LIBRARY
3 5899 00103 2642
W9-AAY-852

# A First-Start Easy Reader

This easy reader contains only 43 different words, repeated often to help the young reader develop word recognition and interest in reading.

Basic word list for *You Look Funny!*

a
an
and
are
bear
coat
day
ears
elephant
floppy
friend
funny
happy
have
he
his
it
lion
long
look
looked
made
met
not
now
off
on
one
panda
put
said
so
stripes
tail
the
them
then
took
was
way
with
you
zebra

# You Look Funny!

Written by Joy Kim

Illustrated by Patti Boyd

FISKE PUBLIC LIBRARY
110 RANDALL ROAD
P.O. BOX 340
WRENTHAM, MA 02093

Troll Associates

*Library of Congress Cataloging in Publication Data*

Kim, Joy.
You look funny!

Summary: Panda learns that "Beauty is in the eye of the beholder" when he is criticized for his appearance by all the animals except his own kind.
[1. Pandas—Fiction] I. Boyd, Patti, ill.
II. Title.
PZ7.K5597Yo 1987 [E] 86-30839
ISBN 0-8167-0976-9 (lib. bdg.)
ISBN 0-8167-0977-7 (pbk.)

Copyright © 1988 by Troll Associates

All rights reserved. No portion of this book may be reproduced in any form, electronic or mechanical, including photocopying, recording, or information storage and retrieval systems, without prior written permission from the publisher.
Printed in the United States of America.

10 9 8 7 6 5 4 3

Panda was a bear.

He was a happy bear.

He was happy with
the way he looked.

Then, one day, he met an elephant.

The elephant said, “You look funny.”

"You have funny ears."

Panda was not so happy.

So he made floppy ears.

He made floppy ears
and put them on.

Then, he met a lion.

The lion said, "You look funny."

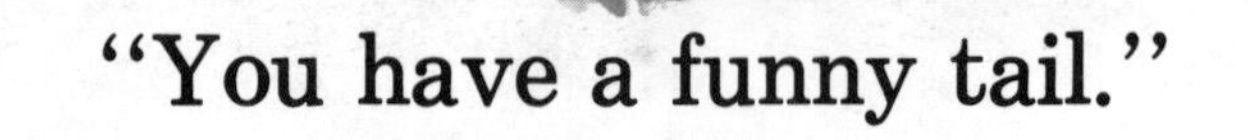

"You have a funny tail."

Panda was not so happy.

So he made a long tail.

He made a long tail and put it on.

Then, he met a zebra.

The zebra said, "You look funny."

"You have a funny coat."

Panda was not so happy.

So he made a coat with stripes.

He made a coat with stripes
and put it on.

Then, he met a panda friend.

The panda friend said, "You look funny. You are a funny panda."

So Panda took off his floppy ears.

He took off his long tail.

He took off his coat with stripes.

He was so happy with the way he looked.

And now Panda was a happy bear.